Sam's Super Family

by Damian Harvey and Paul Davidson

W

"This is my family,"
said Sam.

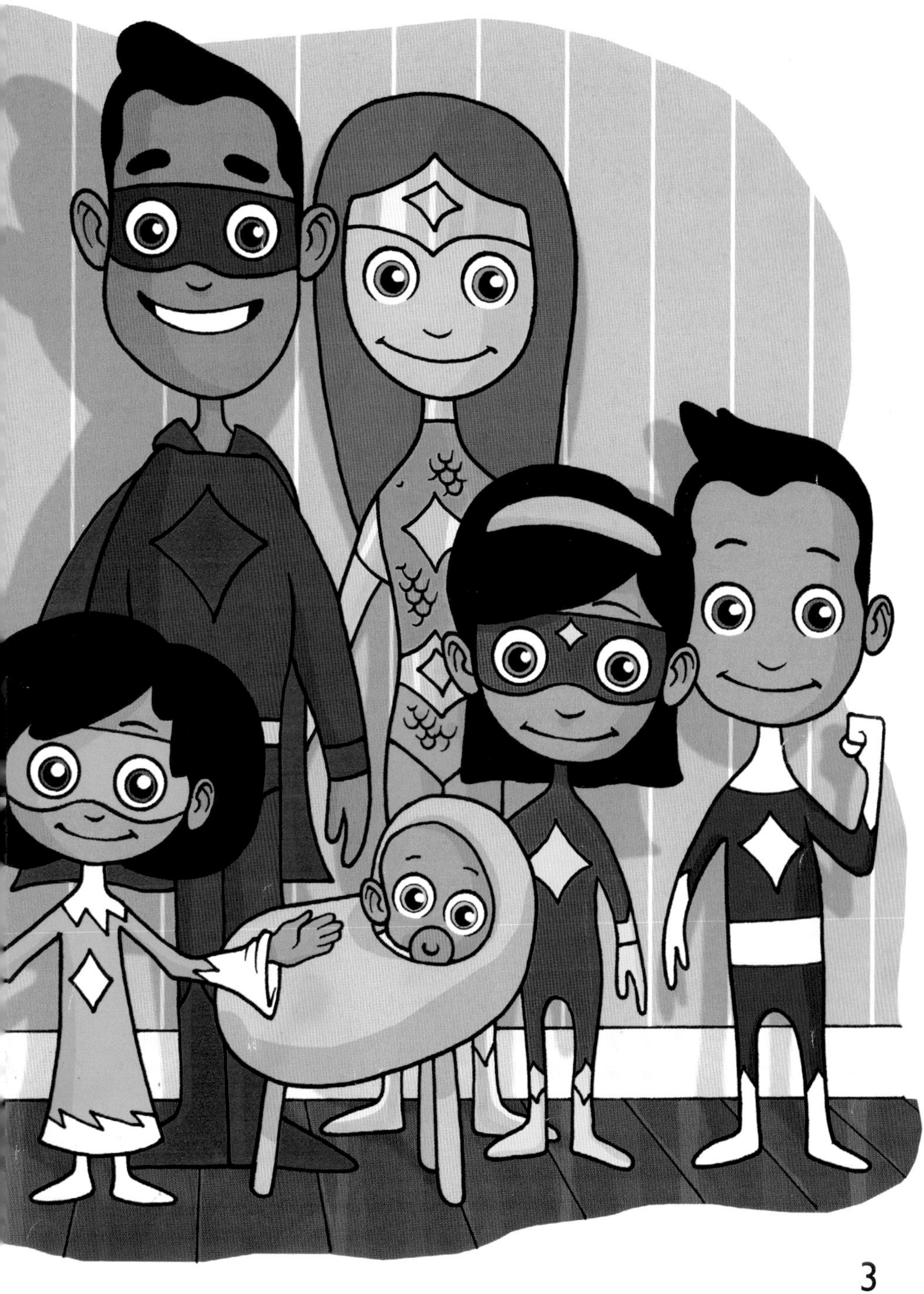

"This is my dad,"
said Sam.

"He likes to help
at the fair."

"Here is my mum,"
said Sam.

"She likes to help
at the beach."

"Here is my gran,"
said Sam.

"She likes to help
on the farm."

"This is my grandad,"
said Sam.

"He likes to help
in the town."

"This is my big brother,"
said Sam.

"He likes to help
at the park."

"This is my big sister," said Sam.

"She likes to help
at school."

"This is my cat,"
said Sam.

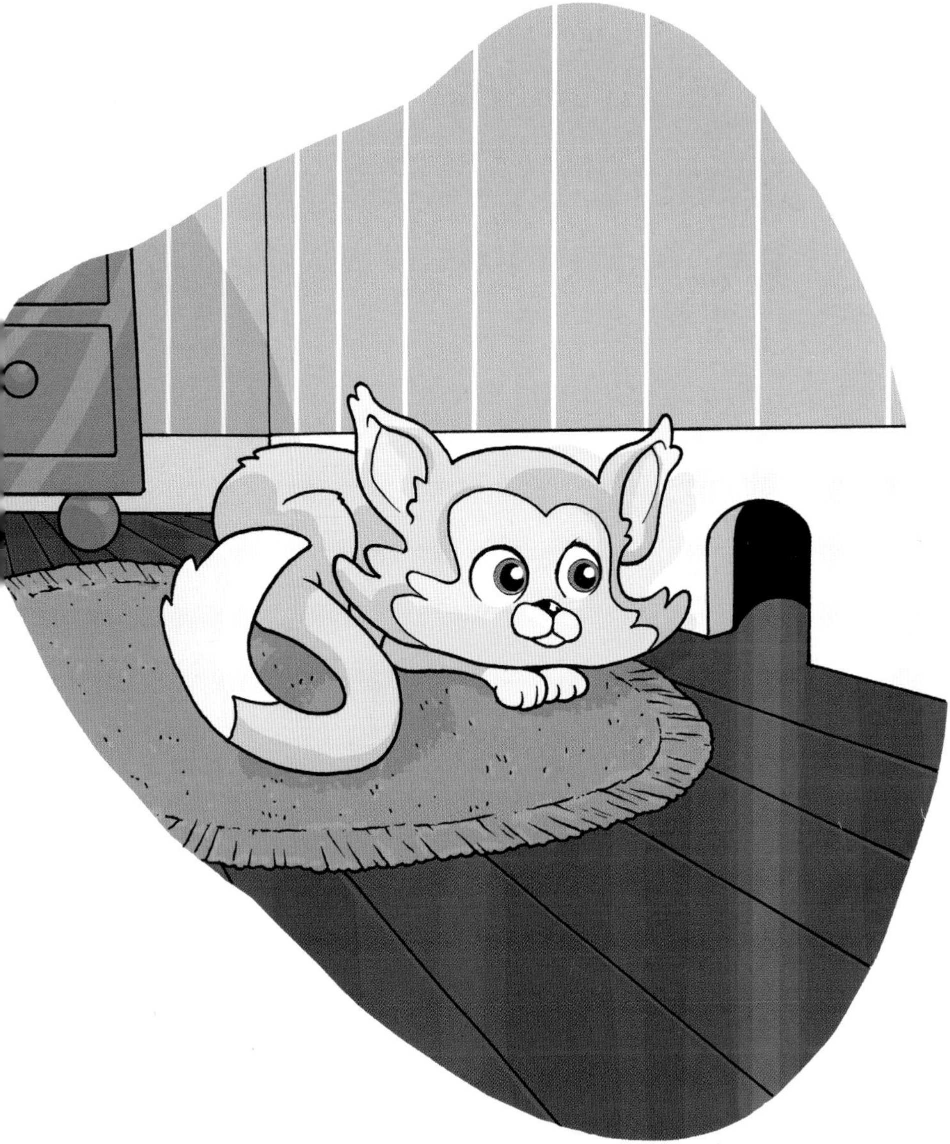

“He likes to help.”

"And I like to help, too,"
said Sam.

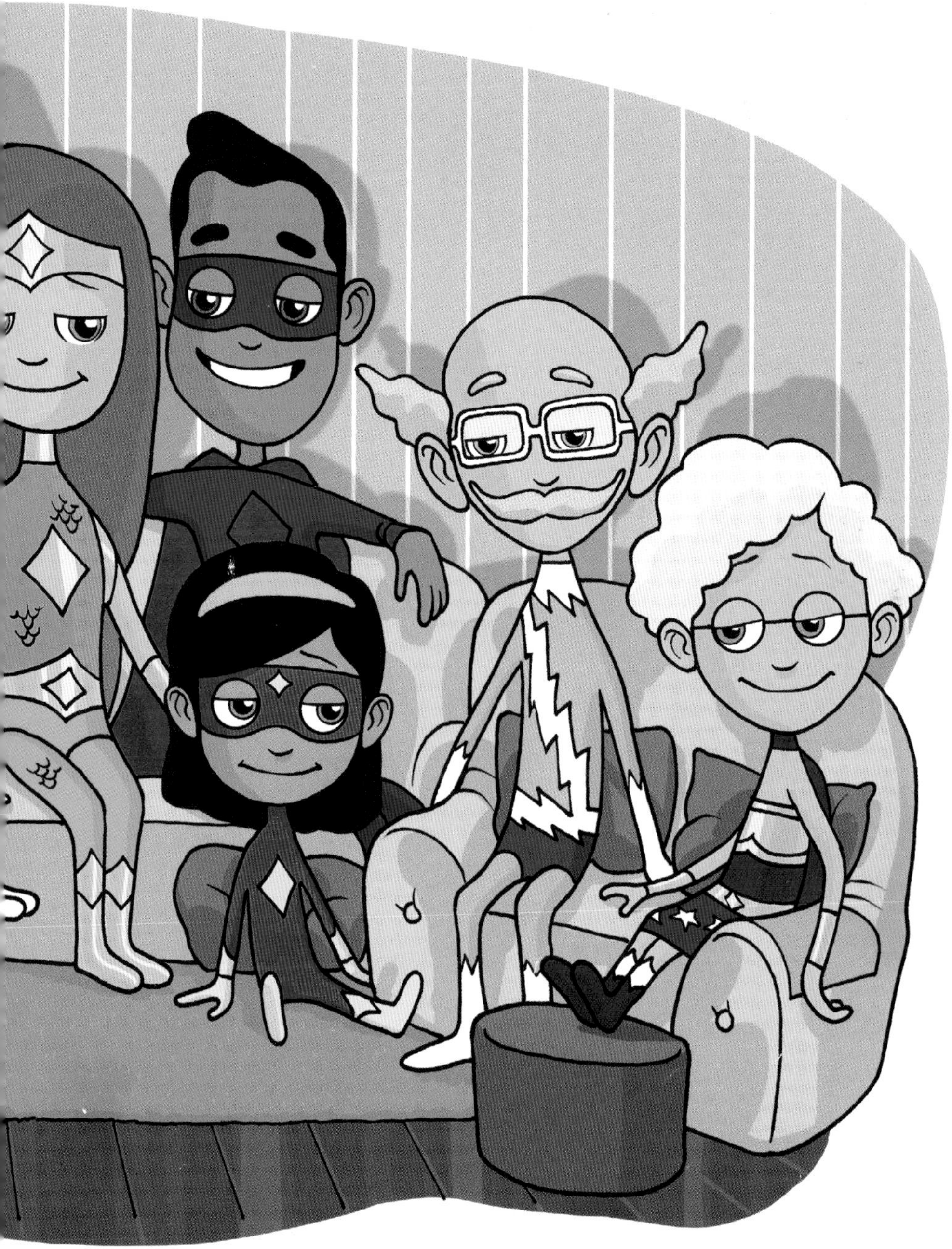

Story trail

Start

Start at the beginning of the story trail. Ask your child to retell the story in their own words, pointing to each picture in turn to recall the sequence of events.

Independent Reading

This series is designed to provide an opportunity for your child to read on their own. These notes are written for you to help your child choose a book and to read it independently.

In school, your child's teacher will often be using reading books which have been banded to support the process of learning to read. Use the book band colour your child is reading in school to help you make a good choice. *Sam's Super Family* is a good choice for children reading at Yellow Band in their classroom to read independently.

The aim of independent reading is to read this book with ease, so that your child enjoys the story and relates it to their own experiences.

About the book
Sam's family is super! They each have a superpower and love helping out. Sam may be too young to be a superhero just yet, but she still loves to help!

Before reading
Help your child to learn how to make good choices by asking: "Why did you choose this book? Why do you think you will enjoy it?" Look at the cover together and ask: "What do you think the story will be about?" Support your child to think of what they already know about the story context. Read the title aloud and ask: "Why do you think the story is called *Sam's Super Family*? What can you see on the cover that make the family look super?" Remind your child that they can try to sound out the letters to make a word if they get stuck. Decide together whether your child will read the story independently or read it aloud to you. When books are short, as at Yellow Band, your child may wish to do both!

During reading

If reading aloud, support your child if they hesitate or ask for help by telling the word. Remind your child of what they know and what they can do independently.

If reading to themselves, remind your child that they can come and ask for your help if stuck.

After reading:

Support comprehension by asking your child to tell you about the story. Help your child think about the messages in the book that go beyond the story and ask: "How did Sam help her family at the end of the book? How do you help your family?"

Give your child a chance to respond to the story: "Did you have a favourite part? Would you like to have a superpower? What would you like to do?"

Use the story trail to encourage your child to retell the story in the right sequence, in their own words.

Extending learning

Help your child understand the story structure by using the same sentence patterns and adding some new elements. "Let's make up a new story about some other places where Sam's superhero family like to help. 'This is my dad. He likes to help at the zoo. This is my mum. She likes to help at the swimming pool.' Now you try. Where will Sam's family help in your story?"

Your child's teacher will be talking about punctuation at Yellow Band. On a few of the pages, check your child can recognise capital letters, speech marks and full stops by asking them to point these out.

Franklin Watts
First published in Great Britain in 2017
by The Watts Publishing Group

Series Editors: Jackie Hamley and Melanie Palmer
Series Advisors: Dr Sue Bodman and Glen Franklin
Series Designer: Peter Scoulding

A CIP catalogue record for this book is
available from the British Library.

ISBN 978 1 4451 5467 1 (hbk)
ISBN 978 1 4451 5468 8 (pbk)
ISBN 978 1 4451 6078 8 (library ebook)

Printed in China

Franklin Watts
An imprint of
Hachette Children's Group
Part of The Watts Publishing Group
Carmelite House
50 Victoria Embankment
London EC4Y 0DZ

An Hachette UK Company
www.hachette.co.uk

www.franklinwatts.co.uk